The Song of the Loch

The Song of the Loch

Sinclair McLay

THE SONG OF THE LOCH

iUniverse books may be ordered through booksellers or by contacting:

iUniverse
1663 Liberty Drive
Bloomington, IN 47403
www.iuniverse.com
1-800-Authors (1-800-288-4677)

ISBN: 978-1-4917-7904-0 (sc)
ISBN: 978-1-4917-7905-7 (e)

Print information available on the last page.

iUniverse rev. date: 10/20/2015

Contents

The Song of the Loch

Our tale takes place off the wild blue shore
A young dolphin happy and unaware
Of what fate had laid at his door
A journey he never dreamed he would dare

Gone be the killing, gone be the slaughter
Our brothers and sisters of the water
Together make the world a better place
Was a dolphin who led the human race!

Old Blue. Tales of the Deep Vol. 7

1

A MESSAGE FROM OLD BLUE

Once upon a time, long, long ago, the whales, the great creatures of the deep, lived on the land with the rest of the warm-blooded mammals. Then, millions of years ago, along with the dolphins and their cousins, the sea otters and sea cows, they left the land and returned to the sea. And no one knows why.

Dolphins are like small whales. Like whales, they breathe air through a small blowhole or spout on the tops of their heads. Unlike whales, they do not sing, but they do talk, by making a clicking noise—*click, click, click*. They also smile.

Wee Bottlenose was a dolphin who lived and played around the islands of Scotland. Sometimes he would swim alongside fishing boats and at other times, he would dive deep to explore strange new underwater worlds and meet strange new underwater creatures.

One day, Wee Bottlenose was exploring some caves. Like all dolphins, he was a bit short-sighted, and so he was using his clicking noises to find his way around. It's called echolocation, a kind of dolphin sonar. If Wee Bottlenose sent out some clicks and the sounds came back to him, then he would know the clicks had bounced off of something and that there was an object or creature ahead.

In one cave though, **Wee** Bottlenose sent out his clicks—*click, click, click*—and nothing came back. "That's strange," he thought to himself. "This cave must be bigger than I thought." It was also very dark. And very cold. "This is getting a bit scary," Wee Bottlenose thought. "There could be...*anything*...up there."

Just then, Wee Bottlenose felt something brush up against him. "Heavens above that could have been anything!" he said to himself.

Actually, it was a salmon. Wee Bottlenose chased after the noble fish, intent on learning more about this mysterious cave, but the salmon neither stopped nor turned. He was in a hurry. You see, Scottish salmon are born in small rivers, swim to the ocean and then head straight to Greenland to eat. Having been fed, they then return to the same small, Scottish river they were born in to lay their eggs in and die. It is a very single-minded operation and so they don't really have much time to swim around and chat.

Refusing to be put off, Wee Bottlenose decided to step on it in order to keep up with the speeding salmon.

"Mr. Salmon, I was wondering if I could ask you a question?" said Wee Bottlenose.

"The name's Sandy" the Scottish salmon grumpily replied.

"Sorry, Sandy," apologised Wee Bottlenose. "I was just looking for some information on that cave, the one you just left."

But Sandy the Salmon swam on, trying desperately to blot out this horrible, high-pitched clicking. He found it very annoying.

Wee Bottlenose persisted. "So, what can you tell me about the cave?"

"Stop it! Just stop it! Those clicks of yours are goin' right through me! Now BE QUIET!" Sandy shouted in a thick, crotchety, Scottish accent.

Wee Bottlenose was a bit taken aback. This was quite possibly the grumpiest, rudest creature he had ever met, but he was determined.

"OK, I hear what you're saying. I promise to click a little more quietly."

"SHUT UP!" shouted Sandy who was being driven mad by these clicks, believing that his head might be about to explode. He felt like spinning round and slapping this annoying little dolphin in the face with his tail. However, Sandy decided the quickest way to get rid of Wee Bottlenose was to give in and answer his questions, and then just speed off toward Greenland.

"Ah've no got all day laddie. So let's just make this very clear, very quick and very precise. It's nae a CAVE, it's a TUNNEL!!!"

"A tunnel ... now that is interesting—*very* interesting! Where does it lead?" Wee Bottlenose asked excitedly.

Sandy rolled his eyes—was there no end to these questions?

"Can ye no just leave it alone? Right. Last and final answer! It leads to...."

Sandy was just about to reveal the exact place where the tunnel led when he was interrupted—not by Wee Bottlenose—but by the song of a whale. A song that had travelled many thousands of miles. The song of a blue whale. The song of Old Blue, the oldest, largest and wisest of all the creatures of the deep.

Calling all the creatures of the deep!
Calling all the creatures of the deep!
Old Blue would like a meeting, please.
Swim quickly to the Northern Seas!

Wee Bottlenose listened intently to Old Blue's message, and then turned to Sandy.

"Right, no problem. We can go into details about the tunnel on the way."

"What way? I'm no going your way, I'm going thatta way," Sandy replied, pointing his fin in the direction of Greenland, which was a bit north, but a bit west, too.

"But Old Blue has requested a meeting of all the creatures of the deep and last time I checked that would include you." replied Wee Bottlenose

3

"You think I'm going to go thousands of miles out of ma way to attend a United Nations of Fish? Sorry pal. I'm starvin'. Bye!" And with that, Sandy sped off.

"Sandy! Sandy!" Wee Bottlenose shouted after the speeding salmon. "Please! This could be important."

But it was too late; Sandy was gone, lost in the murky waters.

2

JOURNEY TO THE POLE

It would take many weeks for all the different branches of underwater life to travel to the Northern Seas. For the whales, there would be narwhals, minkes, rorquals, bowheads, killer whales, and humpbacks. Bottlenose dolphins, different kinds of porpoises, grey seals, fur seals, harp seals, sea-lions, dugongs, manatees, walruses, would all be there and many others too.

Wee Bottlenose decided to swim up past Skye and Scotland's outer isles, and then onto the Faroe Islands before following the cod to Iceland and heading due north. For the first part of his journey, he swam alone, popping up for air from time to time. His only company the odd gull skimming the waves or some seal fooling about in the wake of a long-distance trawler.

As he approached the Faroe Islands though, he fell in with a pod of pilot whales and amused himself by playing with the children and chatting with the adults. One thing was bothering him though: Why had Old Blue called this meeting? He decided to ask around.

One of the younger pilot whales suggested that Old Blue might be holding a party. This idea was gently dismissed by one of the older pilots, who noted that it would be unusual for a party to be held at the North Pole. Yes, Old Blue had hosted parties before, but those were usually held just off Ibiza.

"This is a highly unusual request," explained Amelia, the oldest of the pilots. "Only once before has such a request been made and that was by Old Blue's great grandfather—Grand Blue—many generations ago. This was when the Men in Boats were killing us all. They would kill us with harpoons and giant hooks and then boil our flesh in order to make oil."

Wee Bottlenose started to feel a bit queasy and some of the younger pilots started to cry.

"Amelia," whispered her husband, Avi. "You are scaring the children!"

"Well, I think it's only fair the younger generation know their history," replied Amelia. "You do have a point, however, and I must say, children, that man has since changed his ways. Money was the reason, of course. It became cheaper to drill into the earth for oil rather than drill into us—ha, ha, ha!"

Amelia's laugh was so infectious that she succeeded in making light of this dark tale and everyone laughed along with her. Apart from one sensitive young pilot whale, who swooned and went a little white round the blow hole.

"Well I suppose none of us can really know what is on Old Blue's mind." said Wee Bottlenose. "Until he tells us himself, of course."

"Exactly right," replied Amelia. "Now why don't you swim the whole way with us, Wee Bottlenose. The children adore the company of bright young dolphins like you."

"I'd love that!" replied Wee Bottlenose, both humbled and honoured to be asked to accompany such loving and civilized creatures. "Actually I've never been this far north before and I've no idea what the Northern Seas hold."

"Well, then," replied Amelia. "Let me tell you." She then proceeded to tell Wee Bottlenose tales about giant underwater ice cathedrals, magnificent feasts, and, of course, the might of the infamous polar bear! As he listened and swam and laughed his way north, Wee Bottlenose could not think of a time he had ever been happier.

3

AT THE NORTH POLE

The meeting that Old Blue had called was to be held in a huge ice chamber, deep beneath the North Pole.

Old Blue, as the oldest and wisest of all the whales, started the meeting off.

"First of all, I would like to thank everyone for coming. For many of you, it has been a long and tiring journey, but believe me, I would not have called you all here unless this gathering was of vital importance."

Silence reigned as the creatures of the deep respectfully listened to Old Blue's words. This was of course in one part due to Old Blue's imposing size—Blue whales are the largest creatures that have ever lived on this planet. Bigger even than the largest dinosaurs. But it was more than that. Blue whales also have the largest brains that any creature on this earth has ever had. Far bigger than the brain of any human. Bigger even than the brain of a dolphin, who have the second largest brains the world has ever seen. So Blue whales just demand respect.

"For many generations," Old Blue continued, "we had the seas and oceans of this world to ourselves, free to explore, free to enjoy. But then, the Men in Boats came. All we wanted to do was play in the water, but they took it upon themselves to hunt us. To hurt us. And to kill us. They did this for our oil, which they used to light and heat their homes. The situation became so serious, we could have been wiped from the oceans of the earth. Thankfully, though, man eventually found other means to warm himself and see in the dark. The seas became safer and we were able to grow our families and communities, free from fear and the shadow of the harpoon.

"Recently, however, I have been informed that in some parts of the ocean, these slaughters have never gone away and if fact, in some parts of the world are starting to get even worse."

"Worse?" asked Amelia "We all thought man had learned his lesson?"

"Sadly so did I Amelia," replied Old Blue. "But it is not just the increase in the slaughter of our fellow creatures that I am worried about. Man seems to think it is acceptable to use the oceans of the world as his own personal dumping ground. Some of the chemicals he throws into the seas are now killing us and still it goes on. There are also many tragic cases of young whales and dolphins being caught up in his fishing nets. To make things even worse the sound from the engines on his boats are creating havoc and I am very concerned that if the massacres and barbarity continue, it may be too late for us—for all of us. It will be different this time. Very different, but for reasons I cannot go into just yet. All I can say is that if the killing doesn't stop now, it never will. Please let me have your thoughts on this matter."

Initially, there was a silence, as the shocked creatures of the deep, tried to take in the enormity of what they had just heard. Then Jellyface Jake, a Portuguese man-of-war, made an impassioned plea.

"The time for talking is over! It has come down to us or them! We must fight back! It's time to attack the Men in Boats and kill their children!"

"Hear! Hear!" cheered Shark Attack a very nasty group of man-eating sharks.

"Let's hear it for Jellyface Jake!" shouted Bogieface Bob, a leading whelk.

All around, lobsters and crabs rattled their claws in agreement.

"Oh dear," thought Wee Bottlenose. "This is getting out of hand! All the creatures of the deep with big teeth, big claws, and tiny minds are getting carried away. War will benefit no one. Perhaps I should click up and offer an alternative point of view."

Raising his fin and announcing his presence with a nervous, garbled, underwater cough, Wee Bottlenose managed to attract Old Blue's attention. The dignified elder called for silence so the young, Scottish dolphin could make his point.

"Your Assembled Majesties," he clicked anxiously. "While it is true that some men are cruel and heartless killers, this is not true of *all* men.

"Some men are as gentle and sensitive and intelligent as we are. War is not the answer."

"Hear! Hear!" added a porpoise. "Plus, we wouldn't stand a chance—we'd end up in tins! I've heard that men now have weapons that can boil the seas dry and turn water into air."

This was too much for some of the creatures in attendance. One squid fainted and at least two crabs felt their legs go beneath them.

Although many present seemed to agree with Wee Bottlenose's point, it did little to change the minds of the sharks. They and the crabs started growling and muttering and giving Wee Bottlenose dirty underwater looks.

Then, a manatee started to sing. Manatees are sea cows, which, when they sing, sound like a baby crying. "If only we could talk to man," it sang. "Then perhaps we could convince them to leave us in peace."

"Oh, don't be so ridiculous you whining little sap!" seethed a stingray. "Everyone knows that man does not understand our language. War is the only way. Communication is absolutely impossible!"

"Not necessarily," sang a whale.

"Who sang that?" asked Old Blue.

"I did," replied Humphrey. Humphrey was a humpback whale, a kind of whale that is particularly full of song. He continued:

She who has been silent so long,
Will swim the seas and sing our song.
And men at last will understand,
To us the sea, to them the land.

"What does this mean?" asked Old Blue.

"This is an ancient song of ours," replied Humphrey. "It tells of a creature from long ago, who could talk not only with us, but with the world of men, too. She was the link between the creatures of the land and the creatures of the sea."

"So where is she now?" asked Old Blue.

"No one knows" Humphrey replied. "Some say she is dead, some say she is in hiding. All we have left is the song and the song says she will return."

Old Blue considered the situation. He had listened carefully to Jellyface Jake, Wee Bottlenose, and Humphrey. Now, he had to make a decision.

"I appreciate all of your points of view and I understand your feelings. But now I have to make up my mind. This will not go down well with some of you but it is my decision. We will try to find the creature of which Humphrey sings, but if we cannot find her soon, then I am afraid we will have to declare war. Please swim to the four quarters of this beautiful, blue planet and do your utmost to find her. She is our only hope of peace. May the currents be with you!"

The Search Begins

Wee Bottlenose took it upon himself to return to the islands off the West Coast of Scotland. This seemed like as good a place as any to begin his search as he knew the waters like the back of his fin. Tirelessly, he swam up every inlet and around every bay. He swam in the shallows and the deep. But he found nothing, not even a clue.

Then, just as he was about to give up, he bumped into an old friend of his: Wally the Walrus. Wally was lying on a beach, looking rather thoughtful while twiddling the hairs of his moustache.

"Wally, I was wondering if I could ask you a question?" clicked Wee Bottlenose.

Wally did not answer immediately, but continued to fiddle with his whiskers and stare out to sea as if he was lost in solving some great and important problem.

"Oh dear," thought Wee Bottlenose. "I could be here all day waiting for this hairy, old tusker to provide a response. I'll try and hurry him up a wee bit."

"Wally," Wee Bottlenose continued. "If you were a creature of the deep—which, of course, you are—and you wanted to hide yourself away, where would you go?"

"Where no one would look for me," Wally replied vaguely.

"Good answer, but can you give a wee inkling of where that might be?"

"On the land?"

"Aye, well that's not a bad answer, let's just run with that and see where it takes us...the land...hmm...well, there are rivers, of course, but they're very shallow...."

"What about lochs?" Wally suggested.

"Lochs! Of course! Lochs are like wee seas or in the middle of the land. You're a big, hairy genius, Wally!" exclaimed Wee Bottlenose and off he swam.

Wee Bottlenose then quickly realised that his next step would be to do some research. He didn't know much about lochs, but he knew a woman who did: Selena, Queen of the Seals. Selena lived in a sea loch on the Isle of Skye, a large, mountainous island often shrouded in dark, grey clouds and heavy rain.

When Wee Bottlenose found Selena, she was perched atop a large rock, preening her fur and watching her pups play in the water. On another rock, a uniformed sea lion stood guard.

"Your Royal Furriness," clicked Wee Bottlenose. "If you were in need of hiding yourself from view—in, say, a loch—which loch would it be?"

"One does not hide from view," sniffed Selena. "One bathes in the full glare of publicity in order to serve as a shining example to one's subjects—including cheeky little skinheads like you. Now, please go find a stinking pool filled with rotting fish and take your clicky little speech impediment with you. You are scaring my darling pups."

The protective sea lion on guard began to stand to attention. Wee Bottlenose knew he had one last chance. "Okay, Your Highness, let me put it this way: If a school of killer whales led by Orca of the Atlantic were to suddenly appear behind those rocks looking for your crown jewels, where would you hide them?"

"Oh, that's easy," replied Selena. "One would hide them in the biggest, darkest, deepest loch one could find."

"Which is ...?"

"Why, Loch Ness of course!"

"So, where exactly is this Loch Ness?"

"Loch Ness is surrounded by land," Selena explained. "There is a river that runs up to it from the sea, but men have built a gate or lock across it. For detailed directions, best ask a salmon. In fact, there is a salmon swimming by us just now. Please toss it up and one will ask it oneself before eating it."

"Certainly not!" shrieked Wee Bottlenose. "Some of my best friends are salmon! I'm sure I'll find another salmon closer to shore, but thank you for your help, Mrs Queenie! Bye!"

With that, the cheeky dolphin turned tail and swam off as fast as he could. Now, all he had to do was find a salmon. He had a quick look around, but then, remembering that he was half blind, decided to send out a few clicks to see what came back.

Dolphins may be shortsighted, but amazingly, once their clicks bounce back, they go into their brains and form pictures. So, while dolphins can't see with light, they can see with sound.

The clicks began to form pictures in Wee Bottlenose's mind. He saw a nuclear submarine from one set of clicks, a supermarket trolley with another, then some beer cans, a television set, some more beer cans, a bottle of whisky, some washing-up liquid bottles, more beer cans, and an old toilet roll.

"Oh dear!" thought Wee Bottlenose. "Man is such a messy creature. Why doesn't he clear up after himself?"

Then, one set of clicks came back and Wee Bottlenose could make out, in his mind's eye, the unmistakable image of a Scottish salmon. A salmon he knew. It was Sandy!

"Sandy!" Wee Bottlenose chirped. "Am I glad to see you! How was Greenland? Did you have a good feed?"

"You again?" groused Sandy, his grumpy Scottish accent in full effect.

"Well, pleased to see you too!" retorted Wee Bottlenose, a bit hurt by Sandy's nippy response. "Anyway, I've just met with Old Blue and hundreds of other sea creatures and we have to save them; we have to talk to man. You see, there's this creature that can communicate with humans, but no one knows where she lives or even if she's still alive and, and ... well, there are just so many questions, so very many questions!"

"Right, well, just pick one. I've no got much time," replied Sandy, rolling his eyes wearily.

"Okay ... one question: Is there a way to get to Loch Ness?"

"Why are you asking me stupid questions, laddie? Questions you already know the answer to?"

"I do? Er, sorry, I'm not quite sure what you mean ... are you suggesting that I know already how to get to Loch Ness?"

"Course you do. I saw you there. In fact, I bumped into you on my way to Greenland, remember? I scared the plankton out of you."

"The cave?"

"TUNNEL!!" Sandy barked.

"Yes, of course! I remember now! No need to shout ... so, the tunnel leads to Loch Ness! But I've kind of forgotten ... where exactly was that again?"

"Follow me. But please swim a long way behind me and go and stop that clickin'. It makes my scales crawl."

Realising he had no other choice, Wee Bottlenose followed his new friend, Sandy the Scottish salmon. The sun was high above them, the sky blue, and with his spirits high, the young dolphin let out a click of delight.

"Shut up," Sandy growled.

"Sorry," apologised Wee Bottlenose, who then decided the best way to express his new found joy was not to click, but to smile.

Wee Bottlenose kept this smile up for miles and miles as the pair followed the currents, skirted islands, and dodged the rubbish. Soon, Wee Bottlenose, recognised his surroundings and not long after he recognized the tunnel. It was then that his smile started to fade and fear started to return.

The tunnel was still as dark, still as cold, and, perhaps because this was the second time he had swum before it, twice as scary.

Wee Bottlenose poked his head into the mouth of the tunnel and immediately saw a terrifying sight. It was not real, not something that was actually happening before him, but an image that formed in his mind, something so vivid he would never forget it.

What he saw was something that seemed to have taken place millions of years earlier during a darker, more disturbing time. Horrible, angry creatures with teeth like giant razors were eating each other and anything that moved. One especially frightening beast with big, black eyes and huge jaws was viciously attacking another enormous creature, but this other one was not terrifying-looking. She seemed friendly and gentle, sleek and beautiful with a long, long neck and gorgeous almond eyes. Just then the creature with the big, black eyes turned its head and stared at Wee Bottlenose with a look of pure, liquid evil...like it knew him, like it had always hated him and had always wanted to kill him.

Wee Bottlenose sprang back immediately from the mouth of the tunnel, stunned.

"What's wrong?" asked Sandy.

"I'm sorry, Sandy, but I'm not quite sure I can go through with this. Could you maybe say something to make me feel better? Give me a little pep talk or something, perhaps? Maybe tell me it's all in my mind and there's nothing to be afraid of, I don't know, but ... there's something in there, something ... awful."

Sandy was not at all sympathetic—or amused. "Well, there was nothing in the tunnel when I swam down it. It's all in your mind ya wee daftie. You know what? I've had it. You wanted to know where the tunnel was, I put up wi' your screechin' and I've taken you to the very actual tunnel you wanted to be taken to and now you're freaking out like a scaredy little jellyfish. ... Goodbye!" And off up the tunnel he swam.

Wee Bottlenose's heart sank, the first in what would be a long line of sinking's. He knew there was no way he could ever swim up that tunnel.

"Let's face it, I'm a failure," thought Wee Bottlenose to himself.

"I'll never amount to much. I am a coward and a gutless, lily livered, wimpy little chicken-fish. I do not deserve to have a backbone and I really should return this spine. A creature braver than I could probably make very good use of it."

Just then, the cries of a group of whales caught his attention. Sounded like it was coming from the Faroe Islands:

They're rounding us up! The men in boats!
They're attacking us all, stabbing us where we float!
Nets and knives, driving us to the shore!
The blades, the blades cut us deep to the core!
Blood, blood, blood everywhere!
Help us! Help! Is there anyone there?
Stop! Please! The pain! Stop it, please!
They're killing us all, our blood stains the seas!

Then came the shrieking ... and the screams ... and finally, worst of all, the cries of the young whale calves: "Why? Why? Why do you do this to us?"

And then, there was silence ... the sea went still ... and no whale sang.

That was it. Wee Bottlenose remembered now why he was there: He was there to help, not be frozen by fear and be helpless. He was looking for a way to end the killing. He had no choice; he had to get to Loch Ness. He owed it to all of his fellow sea creatures. There was absolutely no point in being scared or of feeling sorry for himself. So, he revved up his tailfin, rose to the surface, took a huge gulp of air into his blowhole, shut his eyes, hoped against hope, and sped up the tunnel as fast as his flippers would carry him.

THE TUNNEL

Wee Bottlenose's new found bravery was soon put to the test though. There were things in this cold, dark tunnel that no creature should ever have to see. Creatures with bulging eyes on stalks, angry hissing fish covered in electric spikes and some of the longest claws he had ever seen. There were also scaly rock snakes with multiple hissing heads. Giant sudden-death plants all slimy and black, spitting out huge bits of half-chewed flesh that stuck to him and seemed to scream at his bones. And the worms—horrible, stinking, huge black-eyed worms that should never have been born, let alone seen or touched. One even jumped into his mouth and tried to slither down his throat—yuck! But he bravely carried on, fighting back the tears, holding down his own sick.

After a while the water, thankfully, seemed to clear, which although a great relief, soon gave way to his next grave concern. Dolphins cannot live underwater for ever. They have to come up to the surface for air, otherwise they drown, which is an embarrassing way for any dolphin to die. Wee Bottlenose was only too aware of this. He also knew that time was running out. Just at that moment, however, he saw something out of the corner of one of his clicks. The object looked like an oyster and it appeared to be opening ... opening to reveal a beautiful shiny little pearl.

Ever so carefully, Wee Bottlenose poked at the shell with his snout. Then, to his astonishment, the oyster began to speak.

"Listen carefully," said the oyster. "Precious is the pearl. Some say she has been dropped from heaven and caught by shellfish at dawn on the night of the fullest of moons, others say she falls with rain like the teeth of fighting dragons. Valuable is she, for she is the source of all light. But remember this: Darkness, too, seeks her as a prize. Beware Ba'al the Destroyer, but rejoice that Nessie is his foe."

"Nessie?" Wee Bottlenose asked excitedly. "Does she have any connection to Loch Ness? Perhaps she is the creature that can speak not only to man, but to the creatures of the deep?"

"That is one of her powers," replied the oyster, "but she is more than that. She is the Goddess of the Earth, of all life itself, who nurtures it and cares for it and drives it ever on. Many names has she been given and long has she lived."

"So, am I on the right track! Nessie the creature I have been searching for, lives in Loch Ness?"

"She does. You have been guided well. Great good will come of this journey. But beware of Ba'al."

"Ba'al?"

"He that would destroy all life and drag us back into darkness."

"Has he got big, black eyes and huge jaws?"

"Yes. But he sleeps now, deep in the Dark Pool, and will only awaken when you ask Nessie to come out of hiding and into the light. She waits on you."

And with that, the oyster shell snapped shut, leaving poor Wee Bottlenose with far more questions than answers. Heartened, but a little wary, the dolphin sped further up the tunnel. On and on he went, wondering, wondering, if the tunnel would ever end.

Suddenly, something appeared in front of him: a huge, single Eye, unblinking and staring. Then, a booming voice spoke: "Who goes there?"

"Oh, my goodness!" thought Wee Bottlenose as he screeched to a halt. "A gigantic, talking Eye!"

"Aye, aye. Catfish got yer tongue?" asked the eye. "Introduce yerself and the nature o' yer business!"

"Sorry," the dolphin clicked. "I didn't mean to be rude. You startled me. My name is Wee Bottlenose and I am helping Old Blue to find a creature—called Nessie, amongst other names, I believe, in order to save all the creatures of the deep."

"Well, you must be one brave dolphin. All similar have met their maker in this here tunnel, on account of this being freshwater and not salty brine. Your type don't usually last long round these parts. Look around you, me hearty, and take good heed of these here bones and skeletons."

Looking around the giant Eye, Wee Bottlenose was shocked to see the shiny white skulls, spines, and fin bones of many a dead dolphin.

"Littered it is from here on in, with the bones of daft wee clickers like yourself," the Eye continued. "Without salt water, you see, your skin starts to flake, then it falls off till all that's left is your naked little frame."

"Oh, dear," thought Wee Bottlenose who began to feel a bit itchy.

"Aye, it starts with an itch," explained the Eye, "but 'tis not immediate, ye have, on average, one moon till it all falls off!"

"All I have to do is get to Loch Ness and find Nessie," Wee Bottlenose said. "Do you think one moon is enough time? Oh, and by the way, who are you?"

"One moon is pushin' it," replied the giant Eye. "Who am I? I am the Keeper o' the Loch, the Great Loch's eye and ears—well, mostly Eye—and no creature shall pass without my say-so. Address me with my proper name—this is all I ask—and for good or ill, I shall let ye pass."

"Hmm ..." clicked Wee Bottlenose. "All I have to do is guess your name and you will let me through?"

"That's what I said," the Eye replied.

"I need a name," Wee Bottlenose thought to himself.

"Aye, aye. Struggling are we?" taunted the Eye.

The last thing Wee Bottlenose needed at this time was a large Eye with a bad attitude, mocking him in a pathetically overdone pirate voice. Who did he think he was? Jack Sparrow?

Wee Bottlenose quickly came to the conclusion that he needed more information before he could make a guess, so he decided to use a trick he had learned while playing his favourite sport at school: Waterball. He would throw a curved click, a special kind of click with backspin.

Wee Bottlenose would send the click against the side of the tunnel; it would curve around and behind the Eye, and if it came into contact with anything, the click would come spinning back. He sent out the curved click and it did indeed spin back, helping to form a picture in his mind of what looked like ... a very long tail. So, there was apparently more to this Eye than met the eye.

"Hurry up!" growled the Eye. "I don't have all day!"

"Okay," thought Wee Bottlenose.

"He has a long tail, but I can see the skin on the tail is not scaly. It looks a bit ... leathery."

"I tell you what," said the Eye. "I'll give you a clue my name is Elver the One-Eyed ... what?"

"Elver ... Elver," thought Wee Bottlenose. "Elver. I'm sure I came across the word Elver in my *Encyclopedia Dolphicanus*. Elver ... a young ... a young ... eel. That's it!"

"Okay," Wee Bottlenose clicked. "I've got it: Your name is Elver the One-Eyed Eel!"

"No, sorry. Wroooong!" said the Eye. "My correct title is Elver the One-Eyed Elver. I'm still quite young. Bye! Time to go home!"

"Oh, come on!" Wee Bottlenose clicked. "That's cheating! You don't look that young. Surely Elver the One-Eyed Eel is close enough."

"Nope. Sorry. Got to be spot on, Bye!"

"Right," thought Wee Bottlenose who was starting to get annoyed with these stupid games "If that's the way you want to play it."

"Oh, my goodness! What in the name of all the oceans is that?" he clicked loudly while peering into a chamber in the tunnel off to Elver's right.

Taken in by the dolphin's trick, Elver immediately turned to look into the chamber to see what all the fuss was about and the second he did, Wee Bottlenose took advantage. He sped up the other side of Elver, past his long tail, and up and along the tunnel, permitting himself a wee smile at how easy it had been to fool that stupid one-eyed eel—or elver, or whatever it was.

Faster and faster he swam up the tunnel, fully aware that he needed to find some air soon. Just when he was using his last gasp of oxygen and it seemed all was lost, he noticed, even with his poor dolphin eyesight, what looked like a shimmering light, a light that seemed to grow brighter with every flap of his fin. Could this be the light at the end of the tunnel?

LOCH NESS

Loch Ness is the largest body of water in the whole of Scotland. It is also the deepest. So deep, in fact, that it could hold all of the world's secrets and never have to tell. Not only is the loch massive and deep, it is also dark. So dark that that the sun might hide there, ask all the stars to join it, and no one would ever know.

Wee Bottlenose shot out of the tunnel near the surface of the loch, flying and spinning through the choppy waves whilst taking huge gulps of air. It had been a long journey and in any other circumstance, Wee Bottlenose would have earned a long, relaxing rest.

But he knew that time was short. Flakes were beginning to appear on his skin and as he looked up into the heavens and noticed the sun slipping behind a large mountain and the moon start its journey across the sky, he remembered Elver the One-Eyed Elver's words of warning: "One moon is pushin' it!" Wee Bottlenose immediately dived deep down into the loch. Down ... down ... deeper ... down ... darker ... down.

"What great luck," he thought. "No other creature could search these dark waters. Eyes would be blind here. This search needs a creature like me, a creature that uses echolocation, uses sound and not light to see its way around."

But just then, the dolphin felt something scrape against his fin. Not just *something*, a *few* things. Turning quickly in fright, he sent out a click to see who or what this was and to his amazement, discovered a family of bats. Wee Bottlenose knew that bats also used sound to find their way around, but he didn't know there was such a thing as underwater bats.

"I didn't realize you guys were a thing! I didn't know creatures like you existed in the deep!" he exclaimed.

"We haven't been discovered yet," chirped a baby aquabat. "That's about to change, however. We've been followed about by a camera crew all week. It's a big National Geographic/ BBC co-production. Soon, the place will be crawling with bat-watchers. It's all a bit annoying, far too much fuss, so we thought we'd get away from it for a bit. We have a holiday cave near here, but now it's time to go to the Faroe Islands for the Gathering."

"Well, I hope the humans don't spoil your peace too much," clicked Wee Bottlenose. "Speaking of which, I don't suppose you've come across a large creature, talks with both humans and marine life ... goes by the name of Nessie?"

"Nessie! Of course we know Nessie! She's been here since the end of the last ice age—that's when Loch Ness was formed, you know. You'll find her near the giant gate that runs across the bottom of the loch. I think she's a bit shy. We've tried to encourage her to join us on some of our travels, but she says the time is not right; she's waiting for a message from someone called Old Blue."

"Well, that's why I'm here! I'm here to deliver a message from Old Blue."

"You are? Well, please pass on our regards. Any friend of Nessie's is a friend of ours. And if there's anything you ever need, don't hesitate to ask!"

"Well, there might be one thing ... camera crew? Please tell me: What is a camera crew?"

"Man has a thing called television. It's a device that helps men, wherever they are, to all be able to see the same thing at the same time, no matter where it is happening."

"Now that is interesting," said Wee Bottlenose. "I have always thought that not all men are bad and that maybe, just maybe, if all men could see what is being carried out in their name by just a few bloodthirsty idiots, then they might come to their senses. So, I'm thinking maybe this 'television' thing could come in useful for what I believe may be happening in this horrible, dark place called the Faroe Islands. If that's the case, I may need your assistance."

"Of course," one of the aquabats replied. "We'd be happy to help."

"Thank you! Goodbye!" Wee Bottlenose said as he swam off. Through the night he travelled, passing trout, minnows, and sticklebacks, smiling as he went, sending out little clicks of joy.

Finally, he saw something ... something moving ... something large ... something enormous, in fact ... something megasaurasly, massively massive. Surely, this ... must be Nessie.

NESSIE

There are some times in life when you must act before you think—it's a good way to find out something quickly for sure instead of going over and over it in your mind—so, without a second thought, Wee Bottlenose dashed off after the huge creature. Nipping between rocks and old logs and underwater ferns, Wee Bottlenose managed to stay on its tail. But then, he lost track of it. Beginning to panic, he started sending out clicks this way and that, but there was no echo at all. Where could the beast have gone? Wee Bottlenose needed help—and fast!

"Excuse me," he clicked to a strange-looking, glowing loch urchin. "Have you seen a huge creature, able to speak to the likes of us, but also men?"

"She went that a way," replied the urchin, pointing to a huge pile of old bones.

"Oh, my goodness!" clicked Wee Bottlenose. "That was a sudden death!"

"No, no," the little brown urchin corrected. "Those aren't her bones. That's just stuff that's been leftover from the last ice age; old mammoth tusks and the like."

"Her front door's right there," said the urchin, pointing to what looked like a giant arch framed by two huge mammoth tusks. "To open it, just pull on the sabre tooth."

"Okay! Thank you. Bye!" Wee Bottlenose swam slowly up to the door, gave a nervous cough, and pulled on the giant tooth. Slowly, the great door creaked open and the young dolphin peered inside. A strange, green glow greeted him. Then, a voice, sweet and clear.

"Wee Bottlenose, I have been waiting for you."

Shocked, Wee Bottlenose sent out a few clicks in the direction of the voice and when they came bouncing back, he was stunned by the image he saw: An enormous creature with a massive body and a long, long neck on top of which sat a smallish head, framing beautiful, almond-shaped eyes—just like the creature he had seen in his vision at the mouth of the tunnel—the one fighting with Ba'al!

Lost for clicks, Wee Bottlenose sat still in the water, trying to take in what he was seeing. He glanced into her eyes and realised there was no need to be frightened; her look was kind and reassuring and a tiny smile played across her lips.

"Me? You've been waiting for me?" he said, finally managing to eke out a few squeaky, mumbling clicks.

For longer than you can know," came her reply. "Before you were born, Before the cold seas did warm, Before the first winds did blow."

Wee Bottlenose just stared, clickless. Nessie continued:

Without you, this a very different Earth,
A tale precious, little known, rarely told.
Time has come to play your part, prove your worth,
For now the drama cries out for the bold.

"*Bold*?" thought Wee Bottlenose. He'd been called many things in his life, but never bold. The fact that this compliment came from such a creature filled him with pride. Nessie went on:

The world is balanced, at a turning point.
Those that keep us back, hold them to account.

Trust in me and you will not disappoint!

Wee Bottlenose felt a tingle run up his spine, gently reminding him that he actually had one. This was truly inspirational, but if he was going to be completely honest with himself, he would have to admit that although these fine words made some sort of sense to him, they did not make complete sense.

Almost as if the giant creature could sense his confusion, she looked at him, smiled sweetly, and said:

I am that of which the pearl did speak,
Goddess of the Earth, the Bringer of Light.
I have other names: for what it's worth.
My role is to give you strength for the coming fight.
Now, head true north, wake man from his sleep,
And take your place as a Hero of the Deep!

And with that she was gone.

"Nessie! Nessie! ... Please! Please!" Wee Bottlenose cried after her.

There was no answer, but at least he had been given very clear instructions: head north. This idea didn't exactly fill Wee Bottlenose with joy and he felt a shiver pass through him at the thought of the long journey back. Then, he felt another bit of his skin flake off. There was no point in even thinking about it. He was running out of time and he had to get back to the ocean.

Sandy has a Change of Heart

Meanwhile, high on a nearby hill, Sandy the Salmon nestled himself into the pebbles at the bottom of a mountain stream. It was the same place in the same stream where he had been born and the journey of his life had begun.

Now, he was home and ready to die. As he lay there looking back over his short life, however, he couldn't help but remember Wee Bottlenose, the young, annoying dolphin on a mission to save all the creatures of the deep. Now that, was an adventure!

As Sandy shut his eyes and prepared to die, it struck him: Why couldn't *he* have done something exciting like that? Why had his life been so boring—one trip to Greenland and then straight back? Did it have to be that way? Probably not, Sandy thought to himself, but he was a salmon and he did what all salmon did. Salmon didn't do choices or have adventures, they just went home, lay down, and died.

"Oh well, nothing I can do about it now," Sandy thought as he gave out his last breath. But, as he did, a tiny egg attached itself to him under one of his scales. It was an oyster egg.

Oysters are born in rivers on land, teeny tiny and millions at a time. They then attach themselves to a nearby fish and hitch a ride. But why would a young oyster seed, the size of a pin tip, hitch a ride with a salmon that had just lain down to die? If it was like any other of the millions of eggs just laid by the mother oyster nearby, then it would be very unlucky, because it would never reach the sea. This was no ordinary oyster egg though. This oyster egg was rather special, very lucky and yes, it would reach the sea.

Is there any Way Out?

Back in Loch Ness, Wee Bottlenose was swimming for all he was worth. Searching, searching for the tunnel that would take him back to the sea. He knew time was short, so much so that he daren't look up, just in case he saw the moon speeding across the night sky.

Faster, faster he tried to swim, but he felt himself slowing as his skin began to flake and lose its sleekness, making every movement through the water harder and harder. Then, just as he was about to give up, one of his clicks did not return. That was it—this must be the tunnel out! Energised, streamlined, and with his fins tucked in tight, he flew into the tunnel and sped along it.

Then, just as his nose could almost smell the salt water and some faint light in the distance began to lift the darkness and the gloom, he came to a shuddering halt. No! He couldn't believe it! Not now! Not now of all times! It was Elver the One-Eyed Elver! Again! Blocking his path!

"Aye, you again," Elver hissed. "You've got some cheek laddie, comin' back here after your performance last time. Think you could get the better of the ears and eye of the loch? Ye shall pay for that, an' pay heavy!"

"Please, Elver, I meant no offence," Wee Bottlenose begged. "I was on a mission—an honourable mission—to find Nessie and save the creatures of the deep."

"Well, did you find her? Doesn't look like it does it? Nessie! Hello, Nessie!" Elver called out mockingly. "Is that you, Nessie? Ha, ha, ha! Oops, no Nessie!"

"Please, please, please ... I *did* find her! Please allow me through. I have to pass on a message to Old Blue," Wee Bottlenose pleaded.

"No chance!" retorted Elver. "You're a failure and a disgrace and because of your treason, you shall flake and die and join the bony remains of all the other cheatin', lying useless, clickers like yourself!"

Poor Wee Bottlenose. His last remaining strength—his will to live, even—drained out of him and he drifted, flaking and broken, to the floor of the tunnel. It was over: the darkness gathered and the poor wee exhausted dolphin prepared to breathe his last.

Just then, he felt something race up behind him and swoosh past. He sent out one last click to see what it was and saw a speeding salmon heading straight for Elver. It was Sandy!

As if in slow motion, Sandy shot towards Elver, then turned sharply to avoid him and, as he passed, flicked his tail and spanked Elver right in the middle of his eye. Elver shrieked in pain and, temporarily blinded, staggered and lurched to one side.

"Come on, laddie!" Sandy shouted back at Wee Bottlenose. "Now's yer chance! Make a run for it!"

So with one great last effort, Wee Bottlenose pushed himself up, swooshed his tail, and flew past a still-blinded Elver, continuing on and out into the salty sea. He had made it home!

Coming up for air in the ocean, just outside the cave that led to the tunnel, Wee Bottlenose gulped and gulped, quenching his thirst for air. Once he had inhaled all he could and could inhale no more, he turned to Sandy. "So, what happened? I thought you were off to lay your eggs and die?"

"Och I just got bored laddie," Sandy replied. "This feeling came over me that life was quite amazing, incredible even, and that I maybe should live a little more of it. So I went for it."

"Well, for what it's worth, I think you made the right decision—especially as far as I am concerned. Thank you, Sandy."

"Aye, well, any more of your irritatin' clickin' and I'm straight back up that tunnel."

Wee Bottlenose laughed. It was great to see Sandy back to his grumpy old self!

"So, what now?" asked Sandy.

"Well," Wee Bottlenose replied excitedly, "I found her! I found Nessie! Amazing! I'll tell you about her on the way, but first we must let Old Blue know. Otherwise, war will break out. We must make haste. True north, my friend!" And off the pair swam.

The Battle Draws Near

Old Blue, who was unaware that Wee Bottlenose had found Nessie, had given up on any of the creatures of the deep locating the mythical beast that could talk to men. He called a Council of War just north of the Faroe Islands. Swimming slowly back and forth, deep in thought, Old Blue listened to his generals and advisors.

Jellyface Jake was in no doubt what the best plan of attack would be: a full frontal assault led by the jellyfish under cover of darkness. "We slither along the seabed," he began.

"No, no. That's our job!" interrupted a Colonel in the Special Underwater Seasnake Service (SUSS).

"Okay, okay," Jellyface Jake replied. "We slither along the seabed, supported by elements of SUSS. Then we crawl up the waste pipes of the Faroese hunting boats, slide quietly into their cabins, jump on their faces, and sting their eyes out."

"And bite with our fangs," added Colonel Seasnake.

"All right, fine," conceded Jellyface Jake. "There's a lot of biting with fangs as well. Then, once we have achieved this great victory, we send a signal back to the main force, and you all come in and help with the mopping up."

"This is ludicrous!" shouted the commander of Shark Attack, the coalition of very nasty man-eating sharks.

"Jellyface Jake wants all the glory for himself! This is just insane. Old Blue, sir, Shark Attack are the most vicious, hardened, and proven anti-human troops at your disposal. I propose we go in first, smash through their ranks in broad daylight, chew all the humans up, and spit their remains out into the sea."

This plan caused uproar amongst the Jellyfish. But the sea snakes bided their time, sneakily waiting to see who would win this particular argument so they could throw their lot in with the victors.

"Are there any more suggestions?" Old Blue asked, almost having to shout to be heard above the infighting.

"Yes!" wailed a manatee in its baby cry. "Why don't the manatees go in first, sing some lullabies, and lull man into a false sense of security so he falls asleep and...."

Such was the outcry the manatee was lucky to escape with its life.

"Anyone else?" Old Blue sighed wearily.

Avi the pilot whale spoke up.

"Sometimes, great causes require great sacrifices. I propose that a pod of pilot whales go in first. The humans will think we are just visiting. There will be no cause for alarm. Once they see us, they will send out their boats as they usually do. At that point, Old Blue, if you split your forces into two armies, then when the Men in Boats attack us, send one army round either side of their fleet. This will surround them. We will try and hold out for as long as possible and then, we tighten the knot and crush them once and for all."

Avi's plan seemed to win the day. Even Jellyface Jake and Shark Attack grudgingly agreed. Sensing which way the wind was blowing, the sea snakes also hissed their approval.

It was a brave gesture on the part of Avi and Amelia, but it was clearly a highly dangerous mission—almost a suicide mission. Surely there had to be another way?

Wee Bottlenose and Sandy swam through the night in a desperate attempt to reach Old Blue. Dolphin clicks do not travel as far in the oceans of the world as whale song, and so communication, sadly, was not an option. They were going to have to personally deliver the message that Wee Bottlenose had found Nessie to Old Blue. This was not ideal, however, as the trip to Loch Ness had taken a serious toll on Wee Bottlenose. His skin was healing, but not as fast as he would have liked. He was tired and not as streamlined as he would have wished. Would they reach Old Blue before war broke out? Or would they arrive too late. ...

Meanwhile, at the foot of Loch Ness, as the great gate across the loch was opened to allow a large ship to pass, a giant creature positioned herself directly under the ship and swam silently and unnoticed out of the loch. Nessie was making her move.

Almost simultaneously, in a dark pool at the bottom of a huge, undiscovered, underwater trench, on the other side of the world, another ancient beast stirred. For the first time in many millions of years, two great black eyes blinked opened and drank in the darkness. Ba'al had awakened from his long slumber and he, too, was about to make a move.

Hurry! Hurry!

Wee Bottlenose was starting to get nervous.

The ocean had been quiet—too quiet. Just then, a flying fish landed alongside him. Flying fish can remain airborne for over 40 seconds, but dip back into the water before taking off again. In a way, they are skipping fish, but they skip quite fast, sometimes more than 50 miles an hour.

"You headed to the Faroe Islands as well?" the flying fish asked.

"Don't have an exact destination," replied Wee Bottlenose, "but yes, we are headed north. The seas are very quiet today. Where is everyone?"

"Old Blue has gathered a huge underwater army at the Faroe Islands," the flying fish explained. "The attack begins at first light. My squadron and I are going to provide air cover, maybe carry out a couple of bombing runs, too."

"So, it must be war?" asked Wee Bottlenose anxiously.

"Of course," the flying fish replied. "Have you not heard? Where have you been?"

"I've been looking for Nessie, the creature that can talk to men as well as us, and I found her!"

"Did you? Where is she? What did she say?"

"To be honest, she wasn't really that precise, but she did say we were approaching a very crucial time and that I should head north. The important thing though is to let Old Blue know. There may still be time to prevent this war. Do you think you could fly ahead and deliver this message to Old Blue? Just tell him that Wee Bottlenose has found Nessie and that I'm on my way?"

"Yessir!" And with that, the flying fish flapped its tail at the required rate of 70 times per second and flew up into the sky.

"Come on Sandy, time is short," urged Wee Bottlenose.

"Fish wi' wings?" the narky old salmon grumbled. "That's no a fish, that's a bird and that's cheatin'!"

THE BATTLE BEGINS

The flying fish made good time and was able to reach the Faroe Islands an hour before dawn and the start of battle. However, when he arrived and asked to see Old Blue, he was taken first to the captain of the Night Guard: Jellyface Jake.

"So, you have an important message for Old Blue?" Jellyface Jake asked. "A message that could help prevent war?"

"Yes, captain," replied the flying fish. "I must speak to Old Blue."

"He's sleeping just now," the sneaky, old jellyfish lied, desperate for a war. "Can I pass along the message?"

"Well ... I was told to deliver it in person."

"Do you have security clearance?"

"Erm, no?"

"Sorry then. We have to take precautions. You could be an enemy agent. The best I can do is pass the message on to Old Blue."

The flying fish hummed and hawed, but finally decided to share the message with Jellyface Jake. "Tell Old Blue that Wee Bottlenose has found Nessie."

"Thank you, soldier," said the jellyfish. "You are very brave and I will recommend you for a medal ... or decoration ... or something. I will ensure that this message is delivered to Old Blue immediately. Dismissed!"

Of course, in an effort to keep the war machine moving forward, Jellyface Jake never did deliver the message to Old Blue.

When Wee Bottlenose and Sandy arrived at the Faroes just before first light, they were met by an eerie silence. All around them was a huge army of the creatures of the deep. Silent. Focused. Preparing. They seemed to be in some sort of line. The only creatures beyond this point were Amelia and Avi and just in front of them were a number of men in boats armed with knives, hooked spears, and harpoons.

"Look! There's Old Blue!" said Sandy as the pair swam towards the great old leader.

"Old Blue," Wee Bottlenose said upon reaching the whale. "Sir, what is happening? I found Nessie—didn't you get my message?"

"Message? I received no message," a puzzled Old Blue responded with a look to Jellyface Jake, who shrugged as if to say he had no idea what Wee Bottlenose might be talking about.

"Well, I *did* send a message and I *did* find her! I found Nessie! I found her and now there's no need for war!" Wee Bottlenose insisted.

Old Blue looked at the young dolphin as if he wanted to hear more, but Jellyface Jake's eyes narrowed in determination.

Wee Bottlenose was about to continue when a sickening thud met his ears: One of the Faroese hunters had stabbed a hook into the soft, blubbery back of Amelia. Blood spurted from the wound and her cry of agony filled the air.

Jellyface Jake knew this was his moment and seized it. "That's it!" he shouted at Old Blue. "It's begun! We must attack now or the moment will be lost!"

"No, Old Blue," cried Wee Bottlenose, "this is not the way. Peace is the way. *Nessie is the way*!"

But then came another heart-rending scream as a second hook slammed into pilot whale flesh. This time, it was Avi's.

"Please, Old Blue," begged Wee Bottlenose, but it was too late. Old Blue was not listening. A war had just started and events were unfolding too quickly.

"Order the attack," Old Blue said gravely to Jellyface Jake.

"Yessir!" the warmongering jellyfish replied.

Wee Bottlenose's heart sank. He knew deep down that it was too late and the wheels of war were already turning. That left only one option to make sure it never happened again. He knew what to do.

In a cave nestled in the next bay, thousands of aquabats heard Wee Bottlenose's call for help and streamed out of the darkness, swarming up and over an adjacent cliff.

Upon seeing this huge swarm of aquabats, the director of the National Geographic/BBC documentary team, who was enjoying a coffee break with his camera crew, threw down his cup and immediately called for a vehicle to follow the aquabats. They drove quickly to the top of the cliff and looked down over the bay, astonished at the scene below. Two pilot whales were being dragged screaming on hooks to the shore by a number of men in boats. Beyond that, the sea was filled with what appeared to be two armies of sea creatures, one army on either side of the bay, moving forward like the horns on a marching bull.

"Get me a live feed!" the director shouted to his crew. "NOW!"

The entire world was about to watch what was going to unfold.

In all his life of travelling the world and reporting on nature, the director had never seen anything like this, but neither could he have ever imagined, even in his wildest dreams, what would happen next.

As the two horns of the bull began to come together, there was an enormous, powerful surge in the water as a giant creature began to surface, its long, long neck rising tens of meters above the sea. At that moment, everyone stopped and stared, be they creatures of the land or creatures of the deep. It was as if time itself had stood still. Then, the creature at the centre of all this attention, the focus of so much awe, shock, and bewilderment, Nessie—for it was she—turned her almond eyes and gentle gaze upon the captain of one of the boats and began to speak:

Mine the song that has been silent so long.
To us the sea, to you the land.
What I offer is peace, this is my song
Only my words can help you understand.

The captain of the boat looked on in stunned amazement. That was his first reaction. But his second reaction was not one of peace or understanding; it was one of fear—blind, animal panic.

"Fire!" he screamed, and a harpoon flew from the ship seeking its gentle, giant target.

Wee Bottlenose watched in horror as the huge, heavy metal arrow shot across the waves. "No, No, No!" he shouted.

Swimming alongside Wee Bottlenose, Sandy threw himself in a giant leap in order that he may be the target, or at least deflect the harpoon. But his brave attempt was too little too late—the harpoon whizzed above him and on toward its intended target.

Just before the harpoon hit, Wee Bottlenose turned and looked deep into Nessie's eyes, hoping to see a glint of confidence or some sign that she was on top of this situation, that she had a plan to escape at the last minute ... But there was no such look. Her eyes instead had the look of a captain's eyes when she is about to go down with her ship.

But there was also something else in her eyes as her end approached: pity. She did not hate her murderers, she, instead, felt sorry for them. She understood their narrow, animal ways and ... it looked like....she forgave them.

Wee Bottlenose did not know if he could continue watching. But he couldn't help himself and watched helplessly as the harpoon pierced Nessie in the heart just below her long, slender neck. Strangely there was no sound, only silence as the entire, television-viewing world watched in shock and horror and then.

Kaboom!

An explosive charge on the tip of the harpoon exploded and the great creature's long neck snapped back, her eyes rolling shut until she collapsed in the water. The sea reddening around her as the last remaining link between the creatures of the sea and the creatures of the land sank beneath the waves.

Wee Bottlenose looked on in dumb, open-mouthed horror. There was no need for this! No need! Why had this happened? Why? WHY?

Looking up at the sky, Wee Bottlenose noticed that where the sun had once brightly shone, darkness had descended as a giant black cloud drifted across its face. The temperature was also beginning to drop.

People watching from boats, helicopters, and the land shivered and shook, drawing their children closer. Even amongst the Faroese, the enormity of what they had just witnessed, what had been carried out in their name, slowly began to dawn upon them. These islanders were now the focus of the world, their faces beamed across the planet by satellite, camera, and mobile phone, and for all this attention, for all this fame, the only feeling was shame, for this was their blackest day and murder was their name. They hung their heads as one, and many, particularly the children, sobbed.

Save this weeping, silence reigned. The only other sound was the caw-cawing of crows and the gentle, rhythmic lap of blood-stained water upon the shore. There was silence—of course there was, for what was there to say? What could be said? What words were there to describe this crime against the creatures of the sea, the Earth, and even life itself?

Wee Bottlenose looked as if expecting something to happen.

"That can't be it, can it?" he thought. "Surely it's not all over?"

But nothing stirred and all around, life looked darker as if a giant black shroud had been laid across it.

"Come on, laddie," said Sandy, gently tugging at his young friend's fin. "There's nothing more to be done here. No point in dwelling. The world should be a better place, but it's not; it is what it is and she was too beautiful to live in it. Let's go."

Wee Bottlenose could hear Sandy's words, but found it impossible to act upon them, to move, to leave. ... Nessie was magical, unique; she'd been around since the beginning of all life on Earth and now she was gone and the world would never see her like again. It couldn't be ... this couldn't be the end ... it simply couldn't.

"Sorry, Sandy, I can't go," Wee Bottlenose replied. "I have to stay here. I don't know why, but I have to stay."

"I understand," said Sandy somberly, gliding into place beside his friend.

The Silvery Moon

As the day wore on, the crowds dispersed. The men in boats returned to port and quietly snuck home, too embarrassed by the international outrage caused by the worldwide coverage of the killing of Nessie to show their faces. Old Blue stood his army down as a mark of respect to the great and ancient creature.

When the sun set over the Atlantic and a full moon rose, only Wee Bottlenose and Sandy remained at the scene of the crime. Looking at the moon, Wee Bottlenose began to feel an overwhelming urge to dive down and pay one last visit to his newfound—and newly lost—friend. He asked Sandy to wait for him before diving down to the bottom of the bay.

At the surface, Sandy prepared to wait, but as the moon rose to its full height, without him even noticing, the tiny oyster that had attached itself to his scales in that high, lonely mountain stream on the banks of Loch Ness, freed itself and drifted gently to the bottom of the sea.

When Wee Bottlenose found Nessie, he was still in a state of disbelief. There she lay, still and motionless. Her face was not twisted in agony, but rather had the look of one who was at peace. Wee Bottlenose took some comfort from this and nuzzled up to her for one final touch, one last goodbye.

Then, just as he was about to give Nessie a farewell peck, one of her eyes opened and she softly spoke:

"Precious is the pearl. Some say she has been dropped from heaven and caught by shellfish at dawn on the night of the fullest of moons, others say she falls with rain like the teeth of fighting dragons. That which was dark will be light. That which was dead will have life. I have one more gift and this gift, Wee Bottlenose, I give to you."

And with that, Nessie's eyes closed, her voice fell silent, and she quietly passed.

Before Wee Bottlenose could know what to think or what to feel, he heard a voice behind him:

This role you have, it must be played out.
The world is balanced, at a turning point.
Those that keep us back, hold them to account.
Trust in me and you will not disappoint.

Wee Bottlenose spun round and was amazed to find a tiny oyster.

"This story is not over," the oyster continued. "You have played your part and you have played it well. But now you must continue your role. The reason you were chosen is the belief that you have shown in the world of men. They are not all bad and from this understanding a bridge can be built and peace can begin to grow. You know you come from the same place?"

"I ... I don't understand," a confused Wee Bottlenose stammered.

"Many millions of years ago, the whales, the great creatures of the deep, lived on land with the rest of the warm-blooded mammals. Then, millions of years ago, along with you dolphins and your cousins the sea otters and sea cows, they left the land and returned to the sea."

"They did? I did? We did?" Wee Bottlenose asked. "So, why did we return to the sea?"

"You were asked to return. By Nessie."

"Why would she make such a request?"

"So that the creatures of the deep and man could come together one day, that the great minds could meet, and the world could move forward, out of the darkness and into the light. You see, if you had stayed on land, man would have killed you all, and then he would never have been able to talk to you and to learn from you. You had to be kept safe so that all the intelligent creatures on this planet could come together and save it from itself. Man is too primitive and could not do it alone. He needs your help."

"That's quite beautiful," replied Wee Bottlenose, "and it makes sense and while I'm happy to help, there is one problem, one gigantic problem: How are we supposed to start a conversation with man about how to make the world a better place if the one creature that could actually talk to man is now, erm ... gone?"

"Often in this life, we look outwards and try and see the big picture in order to make sense of it all," the oyster explained. "Sometimes, however, it is not the biggest that has the greatest power, but the smallest. Sometimes, we should not look at the world without, but the world within. Pay attention, Wee Bottlenose, for Nessie has left you one last gift."

With that, the oyster fell silent and its shell slowly began to open, revealing a tiny, glowing pearl. Then, from this tiny pearl, light began to stream, faintly at first, then in an almost blinding, brilliant beam. Wee Bottlenose, though half blind as he was, could not only see it, *he could feel it ... and it felt like ... love.* Yes, sometimes it is not the biggest that has the greatest power, but the smallest.

Wee Bottlenose turned round and saw exactly where the light was travelling: It was being directed at Nessie. Soon, she was bathed in a beautiful, warm glow and within that glow, from the death and the silence, Wee Bottlenose watched a tiny air bubble emerge and float to the surface of the sea ... and then another ... and another ... and another. All coming from a small opening just below the great creature's belly. Then, the opening began to stretch and widen. Suddenly, to the dolphin's astonishment, a tiny flipper appeared, quickly followed by a second, and then, struggling to emerge, a little head attached to a long, long neck. Soon, the small creature freed itself completely and after stretching and squinting, it looked at Wee Bottlenose with beautiful, familiar almond eyes and smiled gently.

It was a baby Nessie!

"Boy, that's one ugly beastie," said a voice behind Wee Bottlenose. It was, of course, Sandy, who had swum down to check on his friend.

"Look, Sandy," Wee Bottlenose replied, "she's very young now, but trust me, when she grows up she will be absolutely gorgeous."

"Well, I'll have to take your word for that. Hopefully, she'll take after her mother. So, I dinnae mean to be rude, but is there any point to her? I mean can she talk?"

"I don't know. Let's try," Wee Bottlenose said, leaning down towards the tiny, new being. "Hello? Who's a pretty Nessie girl? Hello?"

There was no reply.

"Nothing," grumbled Sandy. "So, we're stuck with some dumb baby Nessie who no one can see the point of?"

But then, to Sandy's amazement, the young whatever-it-was began to talk:

The mother has gone, but the child remains,
The battle is over, the war still to be won.
Together we travel, follow the breeze,
New wind at our back, let's take to the seas!

With that, baby Nessie sped off up to the surface of the bay. Wee Bottlenose and Sandy, lost for words, just gaped at each other.

"She's aff her heid!' grumbled Sandy.

"She may well be getting a little ahead of herself," replied Wee Bottlenose, "but I like her style. Anyway, we can't let her

47

just go off on her own. It's still a big, bad world out there. Come on, Sandy, we've got to go and make sure she's all right. I kind of feel I owe it to her mother. Let's go!"

"I'm no liking this, laddie. I'm not liking this at all."

"So, you're just going to stay here and say no to all the fantastic adventures any salmon could ever dream of?"

"Why did you have to go and put it like that? Now, I feel like I've got no choice!"

"Well, being a grumpy old salmon, you'll be well used to that! Now come on!" Wee Bottlenose swam quickly after the baby with a moaning, complaining, whining salmon in tow.

After catching up with little Nessie, the trio headed off out of the bay and into a warm Atlantic night, bathed in the silver light of a full moon. Wee Bottlenose had never felt better. Somehow, he understood now that his life had a real future and direction—and he couldn't wish for better companions on his journey into the unknown.

The young dolphin drew in a massive gulp of air and celebrated the fact that he was alive. "It's going to be alright now," he thought. "It's all good. In the end, good has triumphed and somehow, darkness has been turned into light."

Perhaps, but maybe Wee Bottlenose should not have been so sure or optimistic, for halfway across the world, a mighty foe was making his way, at speed, across a distant ocean. Ba'al, through his contacts and accomplices, had learned of Nessie's fate just off the Faroe Islands. Yes, he had drawn some satisfaction from the death of his ancient enemy, but hatred and vengeance still burned in his twisted, black heart. A new, young light still burned and had to be extinguished. In order for Ba'al's vengeance to be complete, it was not enough for him that Nessie was dead. No, her child and all its whale and dolphin friends, must die too. ...

Le Fin

Whales, along with many other marine species (perhaps most notably, sharks), play a critical role in the biodiversity of healthy oceans. And yet, as a result of overfishing (most of it being extremely destructive...and much of it being illegal as well), pollution, climate change, etc., we humans are not only wiping out many species of marine life, at an alarming rate, but we're killing the oceans themselves. As Paul Watson—founder of Sea Shepherd Conservation Society says, "If the oceans die, we die!"

What can be done to prevent that? Well, there are at least two things you can do.

1) An immediate action that all of us can take is to join an environmental organization like Sea Shepherd, the world's leading marine conservation organization.
2) The other thing is a little more complicated and long-term, but still absolutely critical nonetheless...and that is, we must all do whatever we can to end greed. The obscene quest for as much money in the shortest time possible, with no concern for future generations whatsoever is, in my opinion, ultimately, what's behind all of the destruction which, at its current rate, is simply not sustainable.

But I have faith in you, the next generation of young adults. You must continue the great work of organizations like Sea Shepherd.

Errol E. Povah
First Officer, M/Y Sam Simon
Operation Sleppid Grindini
Faroe Islands, 2015
Sea Shepherd Conservation Society

It's the action, not the fruit of the action, that's important. You have to do the right thing. It may not be in your power, may not be in your time, that there'll be any fruit. But that doesn't mean you stop doing the right thing. You may never know what results come from your action. But if you do nothing, there will be no result."

— Mahatma Gandhi